This
Treasure Cove Story
belongs to

JURASSIC BARK!

A CENTUM BOOK 978-1-913110-39-0
Published in Great Britain by Centum Books Ltd.
This edition published 2020.

1 3 5 7 9 10 8 6 4 2

Centum Books Ltd, 20 Devon Square, Newton Abbot,
Devon, TQ12 2HR, UK.

www.centumbooksltd.co.uk | books@centumbooksltd.co.uk
CENTUM BOOKS Limited Reg. No. 07641486.

A CIP catalogue record for this book is available
from the British Library.

Printed in China.

centum

A Treasure Cove Story

Jurassic Bark!

By Hollis James

Illustrated by Fabrizio Petrossi

It was an exciting day for the PAW Patrol. They were going on a hunt for dinosaur bones!

'Are you pup paleontologists primed for a big dino dig?' asked Cap'n Turbot.

'I'm ready to shovel!' said Rubble.
'We want to find fossils – bones
that are so old, they're hard as rocks,'
Ryder said.

The PAW Patroller rolled up to the
dig site and the pups went to work.
While Chase placed traffic cones
to keep the work area safe, Rubble
used his shovel to dig.

'Whoa! My shovel hit something!' exclaimed Rubble.

Cap'n Turbot was amazed at what Rubble had found. 'These are a billion times better than dino bones – they're dino *eggs*!'

'Way to dig, Rubble!' said Ryder.

Marshall used his X-ray to look inside the eggs. 'You definitely made a dandy discovery for the museum's diorama,' said Cap'n Turbot.

Later, the pups tried to guess what was inside the eggs.
'I bet they're pterodactyls,' said Marshall.
'Or *pup*-odactyls!' added Skye.

But Rubble was tired from his big day of digging. 'Time for a prehistoric nap,' he said, and his head filled with dinosaurs as he began to dream...

Dinosaurs were everywhere in Adventure Bay! A mother pterodactyl built a nest for her three eggs, but one rolled out and landed in a tree.

A triceratops and her child wandered the hills.

And a giant Utahraptor ate Mayor Goodway's lunch!

Rubble was about to rescue the pterodactyl egg in the tree when suddenly, it hatched! The other eggs in the nest hatched, too! Three small flying dinos zoomed into the air.

Rubble had no time to save the pterodactyls because a train was having trouble with a triceratops!

Rubble sped to the stopped
train and found a baby triceratops
resting on the tracks in front of it.
   'Triceratops are my favourite
dinos!' said Rubble. 'Let's get you
off the tracks!'

Rubble climbed onto the triceratops'
back and the dinosaur gave him a ride
away from the tracks. Then they played
with the mother triceratops.

'You did it, Rubble!' exclaimed the
engineer. 'You saved the day!'

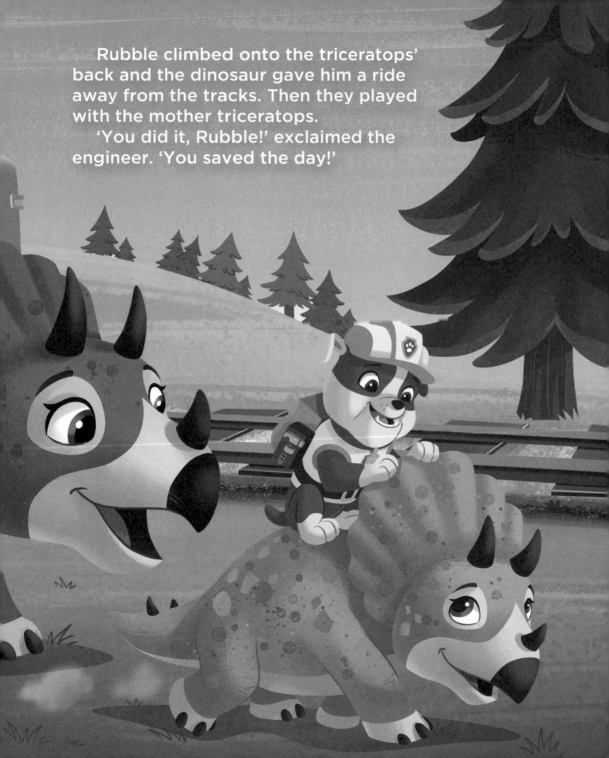

Meanwhile, Marshall found one of the baby pterodactyls in a tree. He wanted to return it to its mother. Marshall climbed up his fire ladder and the dino bonked him with its beak! Marshall fell to the ground.

'I'm good!' Marshall said as the baby flapped down and landed gently on his tummy.

Skye arrived in her helicopter and lowered a harness to Marshall. He slipped into it and, as he was carried into the air, he called to the baby pterodactyl, 'Follow me!' The baby dinosaur flew all the way back to its nest with Marshall.

Over at the playground, Chase found another baby pterodactyl. He launched a net from his pack and snagged it.

Just then, the relieved mother pterodactyl flew down. She removed the net and happily took off with her baby.

Not far away, Skye zoomed over Adventure Bay and spotted the last baby pterodactyl. She swooped down to rescue it – and the giant Utahraptor jumped in her way!

'Keep your claws off that baby, you big bully!' Skye barked.

The giant raptor roared through Adventure Bay. It ate all the hamburgers, then swallowed all Mr Porter's vegetables. It even gobbled up the PAW Patrol's favourite treats, liver links!

Watching this gave Rocky an idea.

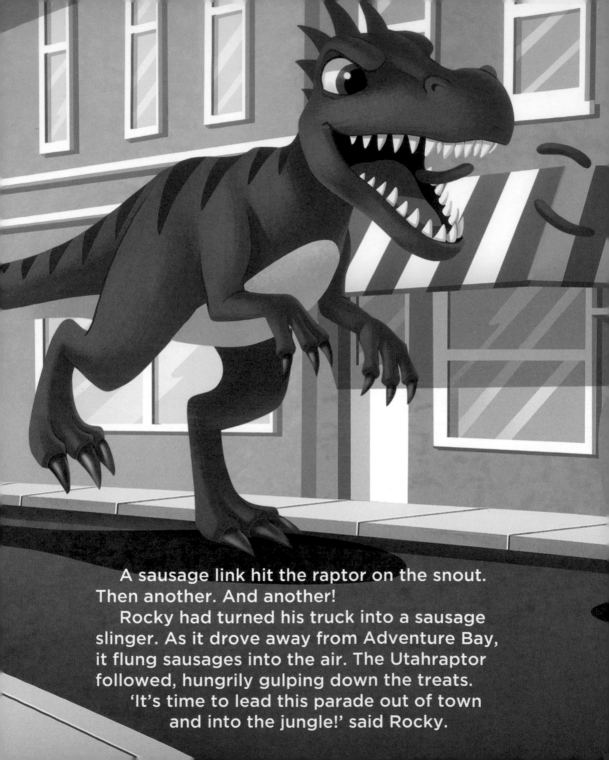

A sausage link hit the raptor on the snout.
Then another. And another!
Rocky had turned his truck into a sausage
slinger. As it drove away from Adventure Bay,
it flung sausages into the air. The Utahraptor
followed, hungrily gulping down the treats.
'It's time to lead this parade out of town
and into the jungle!' said Rocky.

The mother pterodactyl was glad
to have her babies back.
    'We were happy to help,' says Ryder.
'Whenever you're in trouble, just squawk
for help.'
    Skye and Marshall took to the air,
ready to lead the family to the jungle.

'*Aww,* you guys are going, too?' asked Rubble. The mother and baby triceratops roared goodbye as they lumbered away.

'They'll all be much happier in the jungle,' said Ryder.

'Saving dinosaurs sure makes me tired,' Rubble said with a yawn, and he stretched out on the grass...

'Wake up, Rubble!' said Cap'n Turbot.
'Nifty news! Those eggs you found are
from a new species no one's ever seen!
I named it Rubble-o-saurus!'

'Wow! Thanks!' said Rubble. He couldn't
believe a dinosaur was now named after
him. It was a dream come true!

Treasure Cove Stories

Please contact Centum Books to receive the full list of titles in the *Treasure Cove Stories* series.
books@centumbooksltd.co.uk

Classic favourites

1 Three Little Pigs
2 Snow White and the Seven Dwarfs
3 The Fox and the Hound - Hide-and-Seek
4 Dumbo
5 Cinderella
6 Cinderella's Friends
7 Alice in Wonderland
8 Mad Hatter's Tea Party from Alice in Wonderland
9 Mickey Mouse and his Spaceship
10 Peter Pan
11 Pinocchio
12 Mickey and the Beanstalk
13 Sleeping Beauty and the Good Fairies
14 The Lucky Puppy
15 Chicken Little
16 The Incredibles
17 Coco
18 Winnie the Pooh and Tigger
19 The Sword in the Stone
20 Mary Poppins
21 The Jungle Book
22 The Aristocats
23 Lady and the Tramp
24 Bambi
25 Bambi - Friends of the Forest

Recently published

50 Frozen
51 Cinderella is my Babysitter
52 Beauty and the Beast - I am the Beast
53 Blaze and the Monster Machines - Mighty Monster Machines
54 Blaze and the Monster Machines - Dino Parade!
55 Teenage Mutant Ninja Turtles - Follow the Ninja!

56 I am a Princess
57 The Big Book of Paw Patrol
58 Paw Patrol - Adventures with Grandpa!
59 Paw Patrol - Pirate Pups!
60 Trolls
61 Trolls Holiday
62 The Secret Life of Pets
63 Zootropolis
64 Ariel is my Babysitter
65 Tiana is my Babysitter
66 Belle is my Babysitter
67 Paw Patrol - Itty-Bitty Kitty Rescue
68 Moana
69 Nella the Princess Knight - My Heart is Bright!
70 Guardians of the Galaxy
71 Captain America - High-Stakes Heist!
72 Ant-Man
73 The Mighty Avengers
74 The Mighty Avengers - Lights Out!
75 The Incredible Hulk
76 Shimmer & Shine - Wish Upon a Sleepover
77 Shimmer & Shine - Backyard Ballet
78 Paw Patrol - All-Star Pups!
79 Teenage Mutant Ninja Turtles - Really Spaced Out!
80 I am Ariel
81 Madagascar
82 Jasmine is my Babysitter
83 How to Train your Dragon
84 Shrek
85 Puss in Boots
86 Kung Fu Panda
87 Beauty and the Beast - I am Belle
88 The Lion Guard - The Imaginary Okapi
89 Thor - Thunder Strike!
90 Guardians of the Galaxy - Rocket to the Rescue!
91 Nella the Princess Knight - Nella and the Dragon
92 Shimmer & Shine - Treasure Twins!

93 Olaf's Frozen Adventure
94 Black Panther
95 Trolls - Branch's Bunker Birthday
96 Trolls - Poppy's Party
97 The Ugly Duckling
98 Cars - Look Out for Mater!
99 101 Dalmatians
100 The Sorcerer's Apprentice
101 Tangled
102 Avengers - The Threat of Thanos
103 Puppy Dog Pals - Don't Rain on my Pug-Rade
104 Jurassic Park
105 The Mighty Thor
106 Doctor Strange

Latest publications

107 Captain Marvel
108 The Invincible Iron Man
109 Black Panther - Warriors of Wakanda
110 The Big Freeze
111 Ratatouille
112 Aladdin
113 Aladdin - I am the Genie
114 Seven Dwarfs Find a House
115 Toy Story
116 Toy Story 4
117 Paw Patrol - Jurassic Bark!
118 Paw Patrol - Mighty Pup Power!
119 Shimmer & Shine - Pet Talent Show!
120 SpongeBob SquarePants - Krabby Patty Caper
121 The Lion King - I am Simba
122 Winnie the Pooh - The Honey Tree
123 Frozen II
124 Baby Shark and the Colours of the Ocean
125 Baby Shark and the Police Sharks!
126 Trolls World Tour

Book list may be subject to change.